THE DEMONS OF RAJPUR

FIVE TALES FROM BENGAL

The Demons of Rajpur

translated and adapted by BETSY BANG

illustrated by MOLLY GARRETT BANG

GREENWILLOW BOOKS
New York

Published by Greenwillow Books
A Division of William Morrow & Company, Inc.
105 Madison Avenue, New York, N.Y. 10016
Printed in the United States of America
First Edition 1 2 3 4 5 6 7 8 9 10

Library of Congress Cataloging in Publication Data
Bang, Betsy. The demons of Rajpur.
Summary: Retells five traditional Bengali tales.
1. Tales, Bengali. [1. Folklore—Bengal]
I. Bang, Molly. II. Title. PZ8.1.B226De
398.2'1'095492 80-10467
ISBN 0-688-80263-X ISBN 0-688-84263-1 lib. bdg.

FOR OUR
HUSBANDS

With many thanks
to Patti Cehovsky

CONTENTS

INTRODUCTION

THE MAGIC HOUR in Bengali households was dusk, when the lamps were lit and children gathered around their favorite storytellers to hear tales of demons and heroes, sleeping beauties and magic spells. Many of these stories originated in other parts of India and were carried by tradesmen and merchants not only throughout India but to distant ports and by overland caravans to Persia and Europe, Nepal and the Far East. This is why many themes and incidents are common to Japanese and Irish, Sudanese and Finnish, Puerto Rican and Arab tales. India not only originated but exchanged and disseminated the best tales over thousands of years; the main themes of Cinderella and Hansel and Gretel first appeared in Indian stories.

In retelling these traditional tales in English, we have tried to respect the rules of Bengali storytellers. They often mixed incidents around, or used them in new plots, or called characters by different names, but did not invent new incidents or new main characters.

We would like to point out a few of the "classic" themes that recur in the stories, yet are not familiar to Western readers. For example, the seven ranis in "The Enchanted Princess" eat a magic drug in order to have sons, but the two youngest and least selfish ones did not get enough, and their sons had animal forms until their deeds transformed them into proper princes. The peacock-shaped boat in the story symbolizes Lakshmi, the Goddess of Fortune, who, like Venus, rose out of the sea. The cowrie shells and durba grass from which the mothers of the owl and the monkey made canoes for their sons and the vermilion paint with which the canoes were painted all are charms against evil. Ogres who swallow victims whole, the magic cord that connects the hero brothers, enchanted palaces under the sea, impossible tasks that must be fulfilled, the burning of animal disguises to break a spell are frequent in Indian tales. The magical leaf-fruit tree probably derives from the Vedic parijata tree, which rose out of the primal Ocean of Milk during creation of the world; its bark was of gold, and clusters of fragrant fruits sprouted from its branches.

"Neelkamal and Lalkamal" (Blue Lotus, Red Lotus) are typical of devoted half brothers of a good rani and an evil rani. To save themselves from being devoured by a demon, they change themselves into lumps of gold and iron, pure metals which protect against harm. In primitive societies iron was much more powerful than silver in protecting against harm. The demon who demands a daily victim to keep him from eating the sleeping princess appears in several stories. The most important concept in this tale is the life index: The life of each human or rakhosh (flesh-eating demon) is contained in a secret object (insect, fruit, bird, box in a box), always difficult of access, and whoever acquires it has control over the owner's life.

"Golden Stick, Silver Stick" has traditional themes of four friends of different castes, demons who swallow victims whole, the setting of impossible tasks, the life index, and the sleeping beauty. It has a crossroads where four roads meet, always haunted by rakhoshis who can manipulate the directions taken by potential victims. The golden and silver sticks combine the concept of protective properties with the concept of the magic stick familiar to us as a magic wand.

In "The Gojmati" the rubbing of fragrant unguents into the hair becomes an act of black magic when Suworani rubs a pellet of sandal paste into Duworani's hair and changes her into a bird. Here, too, is another favorite theme: the royal white elephant that intuitively chooses the new king. White elephants not only are strong and wise but are associated symbolically with lotuses; in the Vedic cosmic myth, milk white elephants arose from the Milky Ocean simultaneously with the goddess Lakshmi, who held a golden lotus in each hand.

"The Pomegranate Prince" again uses the royal white elephant that selects the successor to an empty throne. The scene in which the hero gambles for his life in a dice game with demons crops up in various countries; in this episode the rakhoshis' mouse turns the dice over so the hero always loses, *until* the hero smuggles in a kitten to scare away the mouse.

Molly Garrett Bang chose the vigorous Mithila style of mural art, adapted it to the purely Bengali *alpana* manner of drawing, and heightened the tempo with finger gestures *(mudras)* from classic Indian dance to illustrate these tales. The Bengali word for stories, tales, and legends is *upakatha.* Storytelling and the drawing of *alpanas* are forms of worship through art which have been the prerogative of women in rural Bengali households since ancient times.

The province of Mithila, in what is now northern Bihar, is the legendary birthplace of Sita, heroine of the epic *Ramayana* and ideal of Indian womanhood. Before bazaar colors were available, the high-caste women of Mithila prepared colors from charcoal, turmeric, flowers, and leaves to paint murals of mystic, romantic, and ritual themes on the smooth mud walls of their houses, developing a remarkable art form full of electric energy and motion while totally without plasticity. *Alpanas* are delicate drawings made with a cloth dipped in white rice-water paste; about half a meter square or oblong, they are drawn on carefully smoothed clay near the entrance to a house. After the artist meditates, she swiftly and skillfully executes a symbolic drawing to invoke the blessings of the household deities on the dwelling and the family. *Mudras* are specific finger positions used in dance and in sculpture to symbolize ideas such as benediction, warning, astonishment, assurance, and protection.

Ours are foreign eyes. We have tried to bring these timeless Bengali art forms across the ocean with minimal distortion and wish only that they could be read at dusk with the sound of cowbells and flutes and the smells of incense and cookfires drifting in across the ponds and rice paddies.

THE DEMONS OF RAJPUR

The Enchanted Princess

There was once a raja of Rajpur who had seven ranis: Big Rani, Second Rani, Third Rani, Middle Rani, Bride Rani, Sad Rani, and Little Rani. He had splendid palaces, stables full of horses, stables full of elephants, chambers full of gold mohurs, and rooms full of gems. He had counselors, advisers, sepoys, and lascars. But still, the people of Rajpur were sad because not one of the ranis had a son, and there was no heir to the throne.

One day, when the ranis went to the river to bathe, a holy man came to Big Rani and gave her a root, saying, "Pound this well, and let each rani eat some of it. Soon there will be seven sons, and each will be fair as the golden moon." The ranis hurried to the palace kitchen. Big Rani gave the root to Second

Rani, saying, "Pound this well so that each of us may have some." She sent Middle Rani to the well for water and Little Rani to the ash heap to clean the fish for making curry. Second Rani pounded the root and ate some of it. She put the rest in a silver dish and took it to Big Rani. Big Rani, Third Rani, Bride Rani, and Sad Rani ate so much that when Middle Rani came back from the well, there was only a speck in the bottom of the dish. The other five ranis laughed when she scraped the dish and licked her fingers.

When Little Rani returned from the ash heap, there was not even a speck left for her. She cried until her tears overflowed into the courtyard. Middle Rani said, "Little sister, do not weep. The smell of the root is still on the grinding stone. Breathe deeply of its vapor, and you may yet have a golden moon son."

But when Little Rani breathed deeply of the vapor, the five older ranis laughed again and said, "If those two have sons, one will be a monkey and one will be an owl."

Ten months and ten days later each of the five older ranis gave birth to a son as fair as a golden moon. But to Little Rani a monkey was born, and to Middle Rani an owl. The raja and the people of Rajpur gathered beneath the balcony of the five ranis and cheered and beat drums of joy to celebrate the birth of the five princes. No one asked about Little Rani or Middle Rani and their sons. They were sent to the Bird Garden, where the ranis were put to work as slaves. Middle Rani had to sweep the garden and feed the birds, while Little Rani gathered fuel for the palace cookpots.

THE FIVE PRINCES grew to manhood. Their names were Hira, Manik, Moti, Shankha, and Kanchon. The owl's name was Bhutum; the monkey's name was Buddhu. The five princes rampaged around the kingdom on their pakhiraj, their winged horses, killing and beheading, always guarded by sepoys and lascars. The people of Rajpur were deeply troubled by their behavior. Buddhu and Bhutum grew up in the Bird Garden, playing in a great bokul tree or gathering betel nuts and fruits for their mothers in the jungle nearby.

One day the five princes swooped into the Bird Garden and saw an owl and a monkey sitting in a bokul tree. They ordered the sepoys and lascars to catch them and put them in a cage in the palace courtyard.

When Middle Rani and Little Rani came to their huts after working all day, Buddhu and Bhutum were not in the bokul tree. Their mothers prepared the evening meal and waited.

Buddhu and Bhutum were amazed by the riches of the palace: the great court, the elephants and horses, the sepoys and lascars, and they thought, "Ba! Ba! Why do we live in a bokul tree? Why do our mothers live like slaves?"

They asked the princes to bring their mothers to the court.

The princes asked, "Where are your mothers?"

Bhutum said, "My mother sweeps the Bird Garden."

Buddhu said, "My mother gathers fuel for the palace."

The princes laughed and jeered, "Hear! Hear! An owl and a monkey with human mothers!"

But one of the sepoys said, "Why not? There were two other ranis at the time when you were born. One of them had a monkey son, and one had an owl son. This is the monkey prince, and that is the owl prince."

The princes scowled. They beat angrily on the cage with big sticks and shouted, "Lies! Lies!" They mounted their pakhiraj and went on another rampage.

Buddhu and Bhutum now knew that they were sons of the raja and that their mothers had not always been slaves but had been ranis. Buddhu said, "Brother, let us go to see our father."

Bhutum said, "Let's go!"

IN THE PALACE the five ranis were lounging on golden divans, having their hair dressed with sweet-scented oils. A servant woman came running in with the news that a golden boat in the shape of a parrot was anchored at the ghat. Its oars were of silver, and its helm was studded with diamonds. Standing in the prow was a maiden as lovely as the dawn, with hair like the monsoon clouds. The ranis all jumped up. Dropping everything, jostling one another, they hurried to see the parrot boat. It belonged to the enchanted Princess Kolabati! There was untold wealth in her kingdom hidden beneath the sea, and the princess herself was bound by an old curse. Only one prince in the world could free her, but no one knew who he was, and thus far every prince who had tried had disappeared forever.

Just as the ranis reached the ghat, the parrot boat began to glide away. The ranis called,

"Oh, Princess fair, with clouds of hair,
our sons would come to seek your hand!
Where is your land? Your land is where?"

From the moving boat the princess called back:

"My land is very far away
with many perils on the way.
Your sons may sail across the sea,
but only one can set me free
from three old hags with kingdoms three,
from Ranga River's dead calm sea,
and he must find the Flower of Pearls
and he must find the Leaf-fruit Tree.
My prince must bring a marriage drum,
and he alone can marry me."

The boat could no longer be seen. The ranis quickly sent messengers to find the five princes and to tell them to return to Rajpur with all speed. The raja ordered five boats, all in the shape of peacocks, to be built immediately. He then called all the people to a great durbar to tell them what was taking place.

Just as the raja and the people were seated for the great audience, Buddhu and Bhutum arrived at the gate. The gatekeeper asked, "Who are you two?"

Buddhu said, "I am the monkey prince."

Bhutum said, "I am the owl prince."

The keeper opened the gate. Buddhu jumped into the raja's lap, and Bhutum flew onto the raja's shoulder. The astonished raja rose to his feet. The people all said, "Ba! Ba!" and stood up also.

When Buddhu said, "Father!" and Bhutum said, "Father!" everyone stood perfectly still. The raja's eyes filled with tears. He kissed Bhutum on the beak and took Buddhu by both arms and embraced him. The people all went quietly away, leaving the raja alone with his two sons. The durbar was postponed for later in the day.

The sound of boatbuilding could be heard throughout the kingdom. The five Peacock Boats all exactly alike were soon riding at anchor, five banners were raised, and the five princes went aboard. The ranis wept and wailed as their sons sailed away in search of the land of the enchanted Princess Kolabati.

When the boats sailed away, Buddhu and Bhutum were at the ghat with the raja. Buddhu asked, "Father, where are our Peacock Boats? We, too, would like to search for Princess Kolabati's land."

When the ranis heard this, they cried, "Shame! Shame! Who do these slaves' sons think they are?" They slapped Buddhu and Bhutum and pushed the raja back to the palace, leaving Buddhu and Bhutum standing at the ghat.

Buddhu said, "Brother?"

Bhutum answered, "Brother?"

Buddhu said, "Let us go home and build our own Peacock Boats. Where our brothers have gone, we will go also."

Bhutum said, "Let's go!"

Little Rani and Middle Rani heard that the princes had sailed away in Peacock Boats to search for Princess Kolabati's land. They said to each other, "Our sons must also go in search of the princess, and they, too, must have Peacock Boats." They went to the river and built two canoes out of betel nuts and cowrie shells, lining them from bow to stern with sweet durba grass. Then they painted each canoe with a vermilion stripe to protect their sons from harm, and set the boats afloat. They

said, "We have lined the canoes with sacred durba grass, and God will protect our sons." Then they returned to their huts.

As Buddhu and Bhutum were hurrying home, they saw the two identical canoes rocking at anchor. Buddhu cried, "Brother, these will be our Peacock Boats!"

Bhutum said, "Let's climb aboard!"

So the two brothers boarded their Peacock Boats and began to paddle side by side. People saw them and called from the banks, "What is happening now?"

Buddhu and Bhutum answered, "We are going to join our brothers!" And they paddled swiftly out to sea.

THE PEACOCK BOATS of the five princes arrived in the country of the three hags. The guardsmen halted the boats and tied them together. The three hags waded into the water, and for three nights and three days they swallowed the seas: They swallowed the princes, the helmsmen, the oarsmen, the sepoys, and the lascars. The next three nights and three days the old hags slept and snored. Imprisoned inside the hags, the princes were sure that they would never see their home again.

On the third night the princes heard voices calling, "Brothers! Brothers!" The princes didn't move.

Then they asked softly, "Whose brothers are you?"

The voices replied, "Take hold of my tail." "Take hold of my tail feathers." One by one the princes grasped Buddhu's tail and Bhutum's tail feathers and were pulled out through the old hag's noses.

"Quiet," Buddhu whispered. "Quick! Slit their throats with

your swords!" The five princes did this, and out came the Peacock Boats, the helmsmen, the oarsmen, the lascars, and the sepoys. They all rushed aboard the Peacock Boats and hoisted the sails. No one paid any attention to Buddhu and Bhutum, who had gone back to their canoes.

The Peacock Boats sailed all night. At dawn they reached the mouth of the Ranga River. Then, as they watched the shore on either side, they saw the land disappear as though it had melted away; there were no banks, no shore, no land anywhere, only water. There was no wind, and there was no sound. The boats foundered. The princes and the crews became more and more frightened. The princes cried out, "Oh, Buddhu! Oh, Bhutum! Come and save us." From across the waters Buddhu and Bhutum came paddling alongside the Peacock Boats. They tied their canoes to the leading boat.

Then Buddhu climbed aboard and called to the helmsmen, "Hoist your sails!" In an instant the boats sailed into the shelter of the Ranga River, where the waves lapped gently against them. On the banks of the river were thousands of jackfruit trees and trees laden with golden mangoes.

The princes and their crews went ashore and ate until they could eat no more. Back on board they whispered together, "Why should we have a monkey and an owl aboard our boat? Let us throw them overboard!" The helmsman threw Buddhu and Bhutum into the water, untied their canoes, and pushed them away. They raised the sails of the Peacock Boats and began to move away up the river. But as they sailed along, the five boats, crews and all, sank slowly into the water until not a trace of them was left.

Buddhu and Bhutum had followed the boats. When they reached the place where the boats had disappeared, Buddhu said, "Brother, something tells me that I should dive down and have a look below. You wait here. I will tie one end of this magic cord around my waist. Hold onto the other end yourself, and when I pull it three times, haul me up."

"Ach-chaa," said Bhutum.

Then Buddhu dived, and Bhutum sat in his canoe, holding the cord.

Buddhu went down, down, into an undersea tunnel. At the end of the tunnel was a marvelous city with a palace as resplendent as the palace of Indra, Lord of the Heavens. But there were no people to be seen—only an old woman, a hundred years old, who sat stitching a quilt made of patches and rags. When the old woman saw Buddhu, she jumped up and threw the quilt over his head. At once thousands of sepoys appeared from nowhere. Buddhu was bound with cords, taken to the palace, and thrown into a dark dungeon. From the blackness of the dungeon Buddhu heard voices around him, saying, "Oh, Buddhu, is it really you?" When his eyes became accustomed to the darkness, Buddhu saw the five princes and their crews. They all rejoiced. Buddhu quickly told them that he had a plan, but they had to be patient, for if his plan failed, they would all be lost.

At dawn, Buddhu lay on the floor of the dungeon, partly covered by a quilt, looking as if he were dead. When the old woman came to bring breakfast to the prisoners, she saw the dead monkey. She picked him up, quilt and all, and threw him into the courtyard. She locked the gate of the dungeon and went away. Buddhu looked around, then picked up the quilt and, staying in the shadows, climbed swiftly to the nearest veranda. He saw that he was in a great three-story house. Across the courtyard, seated in the inner archway of another veranda was Princess Kolabati, talking to her golden parrot. Buddhu swung silently from roof to roof until he stood just behind the princess. She was saying:

"Oh, golden bird, in vain we sailed
our parrot ship across the sea.
No prince has come to set me free!"

Tucked in the heavy braid of her cloud-black hair was the Flower of Pearls. Buddhu deftly lifted it from her braid. The parrot said:

"The Flower of Pearls, oh, Princess fair,
is now no longer in your hair."

Startled, the princess raised her hand to the back of her head and found that indeed the Flower of Pearls was gone. The parrot then said:

"Turn your head, and you will see
the prince who will your bridegroom be."

Princess Kolabati quickly turned around and saw—a monkey! Her head drooped, her bracelets spilled over her wrists, and she fell to the floor in a swoon. Beside the parrot's cage Buddhu saw a wonderfully crafted marriage drum. He picked it up and hung it over his shoulder. Gradually Princess Kolabati regained her senses, but not knowing what to do, she remained on the floor with her eyes closed. Could this be the prince who would set her free? In order to reach her palace, he had had to pass through the kingdom of the three old hags, had had to cross the mouth of the Ranga River, and escape from the old quilt woman and her dark dungeon. He had taken the Flower of Pearls, and the parrot had called him a prince. She opened her eyes and, when she saw the marriage drum hanging from his shoulder, she knew that he must be her bridegroom. She rose and placed a garland of flowers around Buddhu's neck as a sign of their betrothal.

Buddhu smiled and said, "Princess, whose are you now?"

The princess answered, "At first I belonged to my parents. Then I belonged to myself. Now I belong to you."

Buddhu said, "Let us go free my brothers from the dungeon, and then we will return to my country. Our mothers must be greatly worried."

The princess said, "You still must find the Leaf-fruit Tree. We cannot escape from this land until you do. First, however, we must pass the guards at the city gate. They will never let me through if they see me." She picked up a carved chest from a taboret beside her. There were open spaces in the carving, so that even when the chest was closed, there would be air inside. She said, "This is a magic chest. As soon as I get in, I will become very small. Then put the chest on your shoulder. We will be able to speak to each other and the parrot will tell you how to get past the guards at the city gate. Once outside, I will tell you how to find the Leaf-fruit Tree."

"Ach-chha," said Buddhu. He rolled the quilt into a pillow for the princess. It shrank to fit when he put it in the chest. Then Princess Kolabati stepped inside and became very small.

The parrot told Buddhu to hit the wide end of the drum. Instantly a teeming market appeared in the middle of the city. The parrot then told Buddhu to hit the narrow end. The market and all the people disappeared at once. So Buddhu hit the wide end again, put the magic chest holding the princess on his shoulder, and mingled with the crowd in the market. The guards paid no attention to him when he carried the drum and the chest through the gates. Once outside, he hit the narrow end of the drum, and the market vanished.

From inside the chest the princess directed Buddhu. "Go straight ahead, and soon you will see the Leaf-fruit Tree. But go slowly, for there is danger." In the distance Buddhu saw a curious light. As he came closer, he saw that the light came from a marvelous tree. On the tip of each leaf there was a different fruit, and the fruits glowed like gems. But around the base of the tree a huge snake was coiled, writhing, spitting, hissing. Buddhu put the chest and the drum on the ground and ran quickly around and around the tree, binding the snake to the trunk with the magic cord that was tied around his waist. Then he swiftly cut the monster in half. At once he climbed the tree, plucked the fruits, and shared them with Princess Kolabati. The princess said, "Now I am free to leave this land."

But Buddhu replied, "I must first rescue my brothers from the dungeon."

The princess said, "I will remain inside the chest until we are safely in your country."

BUDDHU WENT BACK to the city, hid the drum and the chest just inside the city gate, and went to the palace courtyard. He opened the dungeon door and told the five princes and their crews to follow him to the city gate. He hung the drum over his shoulder, picked up the chest, and then pulled the magic cord three times. At once Bhutum pulled Buddhu and the princess to the surface, and the princes, helmsmen, oarsmen, sepoys, lascars, and all the Peacock Boats floated up, one by one. When they all were aboard, the helmsmen cried, "Pull, pull!" and the sails were hoisted. Buddhu climbed to the roof of the leading boat, Bhutum perched on top of the mast, and the flotilla of Peacock Boats set sail for Rajpur.

On the roof of the cabin of the leading boat, Buddhu whispered to the princess inside the chest to tell her they were on their way to Rajpur. One of the oarsmen heard him and told the princes about it. That night, when Buddhu and Bhutum were asleep, the princes crept quietly up to the chest and opened it. They saw the sleeping princess with her head pillowed on the old woman's quilt. They threw Buddhu into the sea and knocked Bhutum off the mast. They pulled the princess out of the chest. As soon as she was outside, she was her normal size again. All the princes stood around her and asked, "Now, Princess, to whom do you belong?"

She lifted her hand and said, "To the prince who has the marriage drum."

Since none of them could find the drum, they locked the princess in a cabin until they returned to Rajpur.

When the five Peacock Boats landed in Rajpur, everyone was waiting at the ghat to greet them. The five princes led Princess Kolabati ashore. Garlands were placed around her neck, she was sprinkled with sacred water, and she was given rice to eat to welcome her to Rajpur. Oil lamps were lighted and conch shells were blown as the ranis led her to the bridal chamber. They asked, "Princess, to whom are you betrothed?"

The princess answered, "To the prince who brought the marriage drum to me."

"Is it the drum of Prince Hira?"

"No."

"Is it the drum of Prince Manik?"

"No."

"The drum of Prince Shankha?"

"No."

"The drum of Prince Kanchon?"

"No."

"The drum of Prince Moti?"

"No."

"In that case," said the angry ranis, "you will marry no prince of Rajpur."

The princess replied, "I vow that in one month my bridegroom will strike the marriage drum himself."

And so it was decreed that the princess should have one month of grace before she was to be put to death.

Buddhu's mother and Bhutum's mother had wept for their sons for so many days that they felt that their end was near. They went down to the river to drown themselves, but as they walked into the water, they heard a voice call, "Mother!" It was Buddhu.

Then came another call: "Mother!" It was Bhutum.

And two canoes lined with sweet durba grass and painted with vermilion stripes came into view and soon reached the shore. The mothers saw that their prayers had been answered. They embraced their sons. Then Middle Rani and Bhutum, Little Rani and Buddhu returned to their huts together.

The next morning when they looked outside, they saw that at the four corners of each of their huts marvelous trees had appeared. They were covered with leaves as clear as emeralds, and at the tip of each leaf was a delicate fruit. The people of Rajpur came in crowds to see the trees. They could talk of nothing else.

That very morning Princess Kolabati had gone to the raja and said, "Rajamoshai, the month is over, and my bridegroom has not come. I am ready . . ." At that moment a messenger arrived to tell the raja about the wonderful Leaf-fruit Trees in the Bird Garden. The princess looked at the raja, smiled, and said, "That means that my bridegroom has arrived! Let us go together to the Bird Garden." The princess was bathed in perfumed water, sacred durba grass was braided in her hair, and she was dressed in the finest of saris.

Little Rani and Middle Rani welcomed the princess and the raja to the Bird Garden. The princess handed the marriage drum to Buddhu. He struck it joyfully, announcing that the marriage ceremonies would begin the next day.

When the five ranis and the five princes heard what had happened, they bolted their doors and refused to come out.

The next day the people of Rajpur stood on either side of the path from the Bird Garden to the palace, smiling and holding their palms together. Little Rani, Middle Rani, Princess Kolabati, Buddhu, and Bhutum were taken to the palace in royal palanquins. After three days of ceremonies and feasting, Princess Kolabati was married to Buddhu, and Bhutum was married to Princess Horibati from a neighboring kingdom.

TIME PASSED. One night Princess Kolabati and Princess Horibati awoke before dawn and found that their husbands were not in their beds. Instead, the skin of a monkey was lying on Princess Kolabati's bed and the feathers of an owl were lying on Princess Horibati's bed. They said to each other, "My husband is not really a monkey!" "My husband is not really an owl!" They went out to the veranda and looked down into the courtyard, where they saw two princes of Rajpur, as handsome as gods, mounted on horses and keeping guard. Swiftly the two princesses brought the monkey skin and the owl feathers to the veranda and set them on fire with oil from their lamps.

When the princes saw the smoke coming from the veranda, they dismounted and ran up the stairs two by two. Their monkey skin and owl feathers had been destroyed, and now they were free at last from the spell of the magic root!

The next day the people of Rajpur crowded beneath the veranda. They looked at their new princes with wonder, they joined their palms together to salute the happy brides. Buddhu became Prince Budhkumar, and Bhutum became Prince Roopkumar. And from that day on, Little Rani, Middle Rani, Prince Budkhumar, Princess Kolabati, Prince Roopkumar, Princess Horibati, and the raja had the happiest of days together.

Neelkamal and Lalkamal

THE SEVENTH RAJA OF RAJPUR had two ranis. No one, not even the raja, knew that one of them was a rakhoshi. The other rani was friendly and gentle and was very much loved by the people of Rajpur. The gentle rani's son, Kusum, and the rakhoshi's son, Ajit, were devoted brothers. The rakhoshi-rani had a black mind and a blood-red tongue. Whenever Kusum was near her, she became terribly hungry, for her greatest craving was to eat his tender flesh with a savory sauce. But her own son, Ajit, never left Kusum's side. At last her need grew so strong, she cast the Evil Eye on the gentle rani and began to suck away her blood.

After two days and two nights the gentle rani died. The people of Rajpur were overcome with grief. The raja and Kusum and Ajit would not leave their rooms. The rakhoshi was so jealous that she went to Ajit's room and slapped him. Ajit

said, "Kusum, let us never go near my mother again." Then the rakhoshi's mind burned with such rage that the royal elephant fell ill with fever, the raja's horse died in his stable, and the cow died in her byre.

That same night the raja was wakened by a hideous cry that came from his sons' room: "KAIYEE! KAIYEE!" He leaped from his bed, drew his sword, and rushed to them. A monstrous rakhosh was standing beside the beds where the two princes slept. He held the sleeping Kusum in his hairy arms and was about to bite him. The raja lifted his sword to strike the monster down, but at that moment the rakhoshi glided in, plucked a hair from her head, and threw it at the raja. Immediately he turned to stone from head to foot, transformed into a statue with sword upraised. The rakhosh began to bite Kusum, and the helpless statue wept. The rakhoshi laughed aloud.

This wakened Ajit. He sprang from his bed and gave the rakhosh a powerful clout on the head. The rakhosh screamed, "Ai-yee-ee! Ai-yee-ee!" vomited a great lump of gold, and fled from the room. At the same moment Kusum vanished.

When the rakhoshi saw Ajit strike the rakhosh, she was so furious that she bit Ajit. As soon as she did so, she vomited a great lump of iron, and Ajit, too, vanished. The false rani picked up the lump of gold and the lump of iron, took on her own form as a rakhoshi, and flew to the roof. Once there, she stamped her foot and made herself invisible. She flew along the river to a bamboo grove, where she buried the lump of gold and the lump of iron between two bamboo trees.

At the edge of the bamboo grove a crow cawed. From the thicket a jackal howled. The rakhoshi did not hear them. She had gone in search of human flesh.

The next morning there were bones in every house, jungles of bones in all directions. The people who remained alive began to scour the countryside to find the demons and kill them. But when they heard that Kusum and Ajit had been snatched away by a giant rakhosh, they deserted the city of Rajpur and fled for their lives. Only the stone raja remained in the silent palace.

Beside the river the bamboo grove swayed in the breeze. A farmer came to cut the bamboo. He saw a red egg and a blue egg lying between two bamboo trees. They were not snake eggs, but what kind of eggs they were he did not know. He broke them open. Out of the red egg came a red prince, and out of the blue egg a blue prince. With crowns on their heads and swords in their hands, Prince Lalkamal and Prince Neelkamal set out to deliver the people forever from rakhoshes and rakhoshis. The farmer had fainted dead away. When he came to his senses, he saw that the shell of the red egg was lined with gold and the shell of the blue egg with iron. From the gold, he had bangles made for his son's wife, and from the iron, he had the blacksmith fashion a fine scythe.

After traveling many miles, the two princes came to another kingdom. Here, too, they learned, a terrible rakhosh was devouring the people one by one. Every night the raja had to deliver one of his ministers and one of his subjects to the monster. The raja had proclaimed that he would give his kingdom and his two daughters, who were fair as the dawn, to any two princes who could kill the rakhosh. Countless pairs of princes had come and had tried to conquer the rakhosh, but the monster had devoured them all. The princesses and the towns-people lived in terrible fear. Lalkamal and Neelkamal came before the raja and said, "We have come to kill the rakhosh." The raja, who was both full of hope and without hope, gave his consent. The two princes were shown a room in the palace. They unsheathed their swords and sat down to wait.

Night came, and nothing happened. The next night they again kept watch, and nothing happened. They grew very sleepy, and Neel said to Lal, "Brother, I will sleep while you keep watch; then I will stand guard while you sleep. If the rakhosh comes and asks your name, give him my name; do not give him your name." Then Neelkamal fell asleep. Deep in the night there was a knock on the door. Lalkamal picked up his sword but remained quiet. The rakhosh could see a dim thread of light under the door.

Rakhoshes can see only in the dark, so the demon cried, "Put out that lamp!"

Lalkamal said, "No!"

The rakhosh growled, then roared, "Who's awake in there?"

Lalkamal said:

"Neelkamal watches; Lalkamal sleeps.
Neelkamal's sword is sharp.
The butter lamp burns low.
Who dares to come
at this black hour?"

When the rakhosh and his band of demons heard this, they

fell back three cubits in fright: Neelkamal had rakhosh blood in his veins! The rakhosh knew this, and all of the demons with him knew this. After consulting together, they said, "If you are indeed Neelkamal, show us your claws." Lalkamal stuck the sharp edges of his crown through a chink in the door. The rakhoshes gasped, "Your claws are indeed fierce!" Then they said, "Let us see your spittle." Lalkamal dipped the end of his sword in hot oil from the burning lamp and blew it through the keyhole. The monsters jumped back howling, and the smell of their oil-singed hair filled the room. After a pause they approached the door again and said in their horrid nasal voices, "Show us your tongue." Lal put the tip of his sword through the chink. The great rakhosh whispered, "We will pull out his tongue! When I grasp it, all of you pull on me. All together now, PULL-L-L!" and he took hold of the sharp tip of the sword. Black blood spurted all over the room. The mob of screeching, howling demons again surged back. Then there was a long period of silence. In spite of himself, Lal fell asleep. The next time the rakhosh came and asked softly, "Who's awake now?" no one answered. The demons grouped together and broke down the door, toppling the lamp and plunging the room in darkness.

The noise wakened the brothers. Neel, who could see perfectly well in the dark, leaped to his feet. He swung his sword around and around his head, and saying, "Who's awake now?" cut off heads with each stroke. Then he picked up the lamp and lit it, and Lalkamal saw that all the demons were dead. The giant rakhosh was pinned to the wall like a lizard! The two brothers went to bed and slept soundly.

The next morning the raja came to the silent room and

fearfully opened the door. Neelkamal and Lalkamal were fast asleep amid the piles of demon bodies. With a great shout of thanksgiving the raja wakened them, and as he had promised he divided his kingdom between them, and Neelkamal and Lalkamal were married to the king's daughters.

THE RAKHOSHI FLEW back to Rajpur, changed herself into her human form, and descended into the palace, now empty except for the stone raja. As soon as she showed herself on the veranda, her spies came and reported the slaughter of the rakhoshes and rakhoshis by a red prince and a blue prince. She opened her mouth very wide, beat herself on the chest three times, and chanted:

"Oh, poisonous son of my belly!
Oh, sevenfold curse of my people!
My revenge will be sweet!
My revenge will be red!"

She sent two sepoys with shaven heads to the court of the new rajas Neelkamal and Lalkamal. They delivered this message to the princes:

"Your father is dying and soon will be dead
unless he has oil from a rakhoshi's head."

At once Neel and Lal answered together, "Ach-chha. We will get oil from a rakhoshi's head!"

With newly sharpened swords the brothers set out for the land of the rakhosh. After a very long journey they came to the middle of a forest, where they sat beneath a great banyan tree to rest. A pair of bengoma birds had a nest in the tree. The bengoma was saying to the bengomi, "We must find two drops of blood so that the eyes of our chicks will be opened."

Lal heard them and said, "Who is speaking, up in the tree?"

Neel said, "We will give blood to open the eyes of your chicks."

The bengoma came down and pecked their ankles and put drops of blood on the eyes of the two chicks. Then with whooshing wings the enormous young birds flew down and said, "Princes, what can we do for you who have opened our eyes? Wherever you wish to go in the world we will take you." Neel and Lal climbed on their backs, and the young birds circled high above the world. Then, calling "Hoo! Hoo!" they flew over dry land, jungle, streams, rivers, hills, mountains, clouds, sky, sun, and moon toward the land of the demons.

They flew for seven days and seven nights. On the eighth day they landed near a slime-covered meadow at the foot of a mountain. This slippery tract was the land of the rakhosh. Neel gathered some strange-looking peas from a vine and gave them to Lal, saying, "Put these in your tunic. If anyone asks you to eat iron peas, eat these instead." Then they walked slowly toward the meadow. Suddenly a horde of hairy demons came rushing toward them, shouting:

"Hai-yee! Mai-yee! Kai-yee!
We smell blood, Pai-yee!
Human blood! Kai-yee!"

Neel looked beyond them and called out, "Oh, Ai-yee grandmother! Your Neel has come to visit with you!"

A horrid old nasal voice whined, "Hush, hush, quiet, quiet!" until all the demons were quiet. An old hag with long, skinny, boneless arms and wild, matted hair, shaking and trembling, came and took Neel on her lap and panted, "My Neelu! My little one!" The smell of the old creature made Neel sick. Seeing Lal, she said, "Who is that with you?"

Neel said, "This is my brother, Ai-yee ma."

Ai-yee ma said, "He smells human. If he is really my grandson, let him eat these iron peas." She pulled twenty-five iron peas from her nose and gave them to Lal. Lalkamal pretended to eat them, but instead, he ate the ones that Neel had given him. When the old woman saw him eating, she was overcome with joy; he was indeed her own grandson! She took both the brothers on her lap and said:

"May seven kinds of fortune fall
on Neelkamal and Lalkamal!"

But Lal still smelled human to her. Her great red tongue began to drip and seven pitcherfuls of saliva drooled from her mouth. Again and again she was tempted to bite him, but she decided to bide her time.

WHAT WAS THIS dread land which spread so far? Everyone knew of it, but no human had ever seen it. Here the demons who flew by night to seek human flesh spent their days milling about in piles of bones slippery with blood and smelling of decay. Lal looked at the monstrous horde of flesh-eaters and said, "They will destroy the whole world!"

Neel said, "If we do not destroy them, they will indeed destroy the world."

At nightfall all the rakhoshes and rakhoshis flew off to the seven seas to feed on people in every corner of the world. Not one of the creatures remained in the slimy meadow. Neel quickly led Lal down a path, till they came to the edge of a well. Neel said, "Brother, hold my tunic." Then he climbed down into the well and returned bringing a sword and a small golden casket. He opened the casket and took out two hornets. He said to Lal, "This hornet controls the life of all the demons. The other hornet controls the life of the rakhoshi-rani." He gave the rakhoshi-rani's life hornet to Lalkamal and kept the other one himself.

At the other side of the world, the moment the casket was opened all the demons felt a chill wind and became dizzy. They gasped for breath, and their memory began to fade away. In the palace of the stone raja in Rajpur the rakhoshi-rani became drowsy. The hordes of demons began streaming homeward over the rivers and hills as fast as they could fly. Losing no time, Neel tore off two of the hornet's legs. The legs fell off all the demons, but they flew with their hands. Then he pulled off the hornet's other legs, and the arms fell off the demons. But the creatures continued to roll over and over, and swarms of them could be seen coming over the mountain. They were screeching, "Haow! Maow! Kaow!" Just as they reached the borders of the slimy meadow, Neel cut off the hornet's head with the golden sword. The heads of the demons flew all over the meadow.

When Ai-yee ma's head flew by, Lal caught it. The brothers wrapped the old hag's head in Neel's tunic, put the other hornet inside the casket, and went to the edge of the meadow, where they called, "Bengomas! Bengomas!"

THREE MONTHS AND THIRTEEN NIGHTS afterward the two brothers returned to their new kingdom with the news that all of the rakhoshes and rakhoshis in the world were dead except for the rakhoshi-rani. Neel gave Ai-yee ma's head to the two sepoys to take to the rakhoshi-rani so that oil from the old creature's head would save the life of the raja. When the rakhoshi-rani saw the head, she held her own head between her hands and chanted:

"There is no peace
in earth or sky
while those two live.
They both must die!"

She took her own form as a terrible rakhoshi, picked up Ai-yee ma's head, and flew swiftly to the kingdom of Neelkamal and Lalkamal. Arriving at the gate, she said, "Kham! Kham!"

Lalkamal answered, "Tham! Tham!" He brought the golden casket to the gate and opened it. He took out the death hornet.

The rakhoshi-rani saw the death hornet. Her body became weak. Her eyes clouded over, and she fell dead.

The people all crowded to the gate to see what was happening. "Look!" they said. "There is the head of the old grandmother rakhoshi! There is the rakhoshi who pretended to be human. She killed the gentle rani of Rajpur. She came to our kingdom to have a great feast of blood and bones, and now look at her!" Laughing and singing, they dragged the remains of the two demons away and threw them on the ash heap. Then they built a great bonfire and burned them to cinders.

As soon as the rakhoshi-rani was dead, warm blood flowed

in the raja's veins, and he was alive again. The good news spread quickly, and the joyous people returned to their homeland. They gathered in front of the palace, saying, "If we only had our golden princes, Kusum and Ajit!"

The raja said, "If we only knew what has become of my sons!" Then outside the walls of the city the sound of hoofbeats could be heard. The city gates were opened. The raja stood up and said, "What do I see?" After dismounting from their horses and walking hand in hand, Neelkamal and Lalkamal came forward and bowed to their father. The raja asked, "Can it be that you are our Ajit and Kusum?"

The people raised their voices and cried all together, "They are indeed our Ajit and Kusum!"

The two kingdoms were joined, and Lalkamal, Neelkamal, their new ranis, the old raja, and the people of Rajpur lived happily together from that time onward.

Golden Stick, Silver Stick

LONG AGO IN RAJPUR a raja's son, a minister's son, a merchant's son, and a constable's son were boyhood friends. When they reached manhood, they were still close friends, and they often went riding together. However, it was not the custom in those days for young men of different castes to go out together. When the raja, the minister, the merchant, and the constable learned that their sons went riding together, they forbade them to do so ever again. The four friends decided to leave and find a place where they could be free to enjoy one another's company.

They rode quietly away and out of the kingdom and soon reached a crossroads. They agreed to explore each of the four

রাজ পুত্র
মন্ত্রী
পুত্র
সওদাগরের পুত্র
কোটালের
পুত্র

roads for one day and one night and then to return and follow the one which seemed the most promising. The constable's son took the south road, the merchant's son the north, the minister's son the west, and the raja's son the east.

They rode off in different directions, and although each rode all day, not one of them met a single person or saw a single village or even a house. All night they rode south, north, west, and east without turning back. Yet at dawn they found themselves at the crossroads from which they had started! The prince's son said, "This is surely the work of a rakhoshi. She will trap us one by one. Tonight we must sleep at different times so that one of us is always on watch. Now, however, we must search for food, and then we must rest so that our minds will be alert."

The prince climbed high in a tree and lay flat on a branch to keep the first watch. The others went in search of food. They found many different trees along the graveled path, but no fruits or berries and no birds or animals, until suddenly, not far away, they saw the head of a deer. They were out of sight of the prince, and since the constable's son was the best shot, they decided that he should go after the deer. The minister's son went to gather firewood, and the merchant's son went in search of water.

The constable's son took his bow and arrow and crept stealthily closer and closer to the deer. Just as he was about to draw his bow, a hideous rakhoshi reached out from inside the deer's mouth, grabbed the constable's son in her claws, and ate him. Then she ate his horse. When the merchant's son returned with water, he called to the constable's son. The rakhoshi answered in his friend's voice, and again, when the merchant's son came close, she reached out, caught him, ate him, and then ate his horse. When the minister's son came back with the firewood, his two friends called out from inside the deer, "Run, run for your life! The deer is a rakhoshi!" The merchant's son ran toward the tree where the prince was keeping watch, but just as he reached the tree, the demon caught up with him and ate him. She then ate his horse. But when she reached for the prince's horse, the prince stood up, sword in hand, ready to spring on her from the branch of the tree.

"Run, run, escape!" his friends cried from inside the monster. "Now only you can save us all!"

The trees of the forest and the stones all cried, "Run! Run!" and they showed the prince how to find his way out of the forest. But though he ran swiftly, the rakhoshi soon was almost upon him, reaching out with her claws.

As he approached a great mango tree the prince cried, "Oh, mango tree, please give me shelter." The great tree opened its trunk, took the prince inside, and closed itself again. The rakhoshi beat on the tree, screamed, and threatened, but the tree paid no attention. The monster became more and more determined to eat the prince. She planned a way to get him out of the tree.

She changed herself into a beautiful maiden and sat down beside the path the raja always took when he returned from hunting. She knew he would soon be riding by, and so she began to weave wild flowers into a garland and forced great tears into her eyes. When the raja came riding along, he saw a beautiful young maiden weeping as though her heart would break. He fell in love with her on sight and asked her to become his wife.

NOW THAT SHE WAS RANI of the country the rakhoshi devised a clever scheme to get the prince away from the protection of the mango tree. First, she put moldy tamarinds into some spoiled rice and mixed them together until they began to bubble. Then she ate seven bowls full of the brew so that she would develop a fever. Next, she laid rows of dried jute stalks and the stems of dry palm leaves under the mattress of her cot. After that she painted dark rings under her eyes and put rice powder on her face to make it look pale. When all was ready, she lay down on the cot and rolled from side to side, moaning and sweating with fever. When the maidservant brought food to her, the false rani refused to eat or drink.

The raja came hurrying in, asking what could be done, but the false rani only moaned and rolled on the mattress to make the dried stalks crackle and snap. The raja thought, "Her bones are breaking! What am I to do?" The doctors came, and medicines were brought, but she would not take them.

Finally, she said, "Medicines will not cure me. Cut down the great mango tree at the edge of the forest, and let the room fill with smoke when the green wood is burned. Then I will be cured."

Woodcutters were sent to chop down the great mango tree.

Inside the tree the prince said, "Oh, mango tree, your time of truth has come. Please put me inside a mango, and let it fall into the pond beneath your branches." The tree put the prince in a mango and let the mango fall into the pond. A great hilsa fish came along and swallowed the mango.

In the false rani's room, smoke from the wood of the mango tree was blown into the four corners. But the rakhoshi-rani knew all that had happened, and in the smoke-filled room she said, "No! No! It is too late for this. In a pond at the edge of the forest is a hilsa fish. In its stomach is a mango. If I eat the mango, I will be cured."

Fishermen were sent to the pond to cast their nets. Inside the fish the prince said, "Oh, fish, your time of truth has come. Please transfer me into that snail shell on the bank of the pond." The hilsa fish did so, and when it was caught, and its belly was opened, there was the mango, but there was nothing in it.

A villager's young wife came to the pond for water. She saw the snail shell and cracked it open to eat the snail. When the prince stood before her, she was astonished. The prince said, "Goodwife, do not be alarmed. You have saved my life, and I would like to be of service to you." The villager's wife took the prince to the bungalow where she and her husband lived.

As always, the rakhoshi-rani knew all that had happened. She said to the raja, "You have not found my cure at all. In my father's country there are fragrant golden champa flowers, there

are hand-woven mats as fine as gossamer, and there are twelve-cubit melons with thirteen-cubit seeds. Unless these things are brought, I will surely die."

The raja said, "Who knows where to find these wonderful things?"

The false rani said, "In a certain villager's house there is a prince who alone can find these things."

Messengers were sent to the four corners of the kingdom, and finally, the young prince was found and was brought before the raja. The prince bowed courteously to the raja and said, "Your Highness, your rani is a rakhoshi."

The raja became very angry indeed. He said, "Your words are false! She is a true rani! In her father's kingdom there are golden champa flowers, there are mats as fine as gossamer, and there are melons twelve cubits long with thirteen-cubit seeds. You must bring all these things and set them before the rani, or you will be put to death."

The prince departed. He knew who was responsible for these orders. Where was he to find such flowers, such fine mats, such melons? Where did they exist, if they existed at all? After traveling for several days and nights, he came at dusk to a large town. He hoped to find a place to stay, but there was no sign of life anywhere in the town. He searched for some time, and at nightfall he came to a house where a beautiful maiden lay sleeping on a gold and silver cot. She was so still that she looked dead, but there was color in her cheeks, and it could be seen that she was breathing gently. The prince called out in order to waken her, but she did not stir. Then he noticed that at the head of the cot there was a stick made of silver, and at the foot, a stick made of gold. He picked up both sticks, and at once the maiden sat up. When she saw him, she said quickly, "How did you get here? Who are you? Whoever you are, run for your life! This is a city of demons!"

The prince was alarmed. He had escaped being eaten by one demon, and instead, he had arrived in a city of rakhoshis and rakhoshes. He told the maiden who he was and how he had come there. "How can a maiden such as you live in a city of demons?" he asked.

The maiden answered, "My father was the raja of this city. One night a horde of demons arrived and devoured both my parents and all the people of the city, leaving only myself alive. A hideous old rakhoshi saved my life, but I do not know why. Every night just after the sun has set the horrid creatures fly out in search of human flesh. They leave me here, sleeping under the spell of the silver stick and the golden stick."

The prince was about to ask her how they might plan a way for both of them to escape when the sounds of bloodcurdling howling came closer and closer:

"Ai-yee lo!
Human smell!
Suck his blood!
Cook him well!"

Quickly the princess said, "They will kill us both if they find you here. Hurry! Hide in the temple behind the bellflower tree. It is a sacred place, and they are afraid of it."

The demons swarmed into the town, howling, "Ai-yee lo! Mai-yee lo!" The old rakhoshi who had saved the life of the princess came and sat on the edge of the cot, sniffing and drooling. She removed the silver stick and the golden stick and then said:

"I smell a man smell!
Close by he's biding.
Come, little daughter, tell,
WHERE IS HE HIDING?"

The princess laughed, saying, "Of course, you smell a human, Ai-yee ma! I am here! Why not eat me?"

The old creature replied, "I could not do that, daughter lo!" She brought the princess her supper. Then all the demons prepared themselves for sleeping until the sun went down. They poured oil in their noses and oil in their ears and slept right away.

THAT NIGHT THE PRINCESS was again left alone, looking as still and cold as if she were dead. The prince picked up the magic sticks, then said, "Princess, when the demons return, you must get the old rakhoshi drowsy, but you must not let her fall asleep. When she is half asleep, ask her these questions." The princess listened carefully, and when they had made their plans, the prince replaced the silver stick and the golden stick, and again hid in the temple next to the bellflower tree.

When the demons came back and prepared themselves for

sleeping, the princess massaged the old rakhoshi's wrinkled feet with sweet-smelling oil until the old creature became drowsy. Then, as though talking to herself, the princess said, "I am sad because I know that one day the rakhosh will eat me."

Sleepily the old one smiled, her teeth sticking out like radishes, her ears waving like fans. "Hey, rey, golden one! A certain prince could kill all the demons if he only knew how. In the crystal-clear pool there is a pillar of crystal. In the pillar is a seven-hooded snake. If this prince climbs the palm tree beside the pool and picks the golden palm leaf, it will become a sword. If the prince breaks the pillar of crystal and jumps astride the seven-hooded snake, he can kill the snake with the palm-leaf sword. As soon as he does this, seven times seven thousand demons will die. But if he spills one drop of the snake's blood, he himself will die."

The princess said, "Oh, but that will never happen, Ai-yee ma. Does every rakhosh know where every other rakhosh comes from? Are there many realms where demons live? I have heard that in a nearby city there is a raja whose rani is really a rakhoshi. Do you know what her life token is? Do you know what her country is? In her country there are supposed to be fragrant champa flowers and hand-woven mats as fine as gossamer, and twelve-cubit melons with thirteen-cubit seeds. Is all of this true, Ai-yee ma?"

"Oh, indeed, these things are true, daughter lo. The rakhoshi-rani is from this very realm. In the throne room of your father's palace there is a parrot. That parrot is the rakhoshi-rani's life token." Then the old rakhoshi fell asleep. The next

night, when the horde of demons had flown away, the princess told the prince what she had learned.

Together they went to the pool. The prince climbed the palm tree and picked the golden palm-leaf sword. Then he dived into the pool, broke the crystal pillar, and climbed astride the seven-hooded snake. As soon as he did this, all the demons became dizzy, and the whole horde of monsters began rushing homeward, chanting:

"We are flying home lo!
We will eat your bones lo!"

The prince slit the snake's throat with the golden palm-leaf sword. Not one drop of blood was spilled. Immediately the heads fell off all the demons from that realm, and they were never seen again.

THE PRINCE AND THE PRINCESS went into the silent palace. In the throne room a parrot was flitting about, squawking in a raucous voice. The prince captured the bird and put it in a cage. On the dais beside the throne there was a fragrant golden champa flower, a marvelous mat woven of silk as fine as gossamer, and a twelve-cubit melon with thirteen-cubit seeds. The prince gathered them up and asked the princess to wait in her father's palace while he took the magic objects to the city of the raja and the rakhoshi-rani.

He went before the raja and said, "Your Highness, you must assemble your people for a durbar right away." When the durbar had assembled, the things were laid out for everyone to see. What marvels the prince had brought! Then the prince said, "Your Highness, please have the rani brought so that I may present these things to her." The rani's bones shook, and her heart trembled. When she appeared in the doorway, the prince said, "Step forward, rakhoshi!" Where was the rani? Standing in the doorway was a hideous rakhoshi with horrible teeth like radishes and ears like fans. Seeing her long claws, the raja and the people shook with fright.

The prince stood before the rakhoshi and said, "Give me my friend the constable's son, and give me his horse." The rakhoshi looked at the parrot which was in the cage that the prince held in his hand. She vomited up the constable's son and then his horse. Then one by one, as the prince bade her to do so, she vomited up the merchant's son and his horse, the minister's son and his horse, and the prince's own horse. The prince then said to the raja, "Your Highness, now you see that this rani is indeed a rakhoshi." He held the parrot's cage in front of him and said to the parrot, "This rakhoshi's time of truth has come." The parrot squawked, and the rakhoshi fell dead.

The people went to their homes to bathe and put on fresh clothes in order to forget the rakhoshi-rani. Then they gathered again at a great durbar to honor the prince. The raja said, "Most worthy prince, how can we reward you? Our treasure-house is open to you."

The prince said, "I want nothing. It is enough that this realm has been delivered from the demons. My friends and I will now take the princess to our country, where she can make plans to restore her father's realm."

Nonetheless, the raja took many gems from his treasure-house and gave them to the prince and his three friends. Then, taking the princess with them, they traveled home through the peaceful countryside which had been delivered from the demons.

In their own land, each of the young men was joyfully welcomed by his parents, the prince and the princess were married, and the time of countless happy days began for them all.

The Gojmati

THE ELEVENTH RAJA OF RAJPUR had two ranis, Duworani and Suworani. Duworani had two sons, Hemanto and Basanto. Suworani had no children, and she was so ill-natured that she scolded Hemanto and Basanto from morning until night. One morning, when the two ranis went to the river to bathe, Suworani said, "Sister, come let me rub this sweet oil in your hair." But the pellet of sweet ointment she rubbed into Duworani's hair was magic, and Duworani was turned into a golden parrot and flew away. Suworani told the raja that the mother of his sons had drowned.

The parrot flew southward until she came to the garden of a raja's palace. The raja's little daughter was so enchanted by

the golden bird that she begged her father to let her keep it. A golden perch was made, and from that time on the princess always had the parrot-rani by her side.

In the course of time Suworani had three sons. But alas! They were thin as reeds and weak as rags. Suworani fed them rich curries, savory rice, and melted butter, but their arms and legs became thin as twigs. She fed Hemanto and Basanto cold vegetables sprinkled with ashes, yet they grew stronger and taller. The jealous rani studied black magic and sought to destroy them by casting a spell: she collected hemp leaves, dust from a crooked path, and ashes from an old fire, tossed them all together in a winnowing fan, and chanted:

"Hemanto and Basanto, go!
Sons of Duworani, go!
Never to be seen again
in the world of living men!"

At the time that she said these words the brothers felt quite faint for a few moments, but the feeling soon passed. When Suworani saw that she had failed, she worked herself into a fury of hatred. She ripped off her jewels, stamped her feet, tore her clothes, disheveled her hair, and finally lay on the floor and screamed. The noise brought the old ayah running to the room, and when she saw Suworani, she hurried to the raja and said, "The rani is raving!"

The raja come to Suworani's room and asked, "What is the matter?"

"Matter! Matter indeed! Your other wife's sons insult me! Revile me! You must have them killed!"

She screamed until the unhappy raja called the executioner and told him to take Hemanto and Basanto into the forest and kill them. Suworani said to the executioner, "After you slay them both, bring me their bloodstained clothes!"

The executioner led the princes into the forest and asked them to remove their royal robes. Then he gave them tunics of bark cloth, saying, "I cannot do what the rani demands. Dress yourselves in these tunics so that no one will know you; then follow this path until you are far from Rajpur." On his way home he killed a jackal. He dipped the boys' clothes in the fresh blood and took them to Suworani. She laughed with pleasure and hugged her sons.

Hemanto and Basanto walked and walked in the never-ending forest. At last they came to another kingdom. They were so weary that they sat beneath a sal tree to rest. Basanto said, "Brother, I am too thirsty to go farther."

Hemanto said, "Stay here under the tree while I find some water and bring it to you." After quite a long time he found a clear pond. He cut a gourd from a vine, scooped it out, and waded into the pond to fill the gourd with water for Basanto.

It happened that the raja of that country had just died. He had no heir and the people were left without a ruler. As was the custom, the empty throne was placed on the back of the royal white elephant, who was sent out in search of a prince with the royal mark on his forehead. When he found such a prince, the royal elephant was to lift him onto the throne and bring him back to the palace to be the new raja of the country. The elephant had roamed the world from end to end but had found no prince to rule the kingdom. One day he came to a forest where a splendid youth was standing in a pond filling a gourd with water. The youth was dressed in a coarse tunic of bark cloth, but the royal mark was on his forehead! The elephant looped its trunk around Hemanto and swung him up onto the throne.

The astonished prince did not know what to do. He called out, "Basanto! Basanto!" but the elephant charged through the forest and headed for his homeland.

When the elephant reached the city gates, banners were raised, and soon the pathway to the palace was lined with subjects, sepoys, courtiers, ministers, and the resplendent palace guard. They all joined their palms together to welcome the bark-clad prince whom the elephant had brought to be their ruler. The throne was restored to the palace. Hemanto was clothed in the regal splendor befitting his rank, and amid great rejoicing the people acclaimed their raja. The young raja soon won lands and wealth for the kingdom.

Beneath the sal tree Basanto waited and waited. As night fell, he searched for his brother, calling, calling. Then, tired, thirsty, and hungry, he lay on the soft floor of the forest and fell asleep.

Early the next morning, a muni came along the path to fetch water from a pond. The hermit saw a noble youth dressed in a tunic made of bark cloth, lost in slumber. When Basanto wakened, the muni welcomed him to the forest. In the months that followed, Basanto learned to cut wood, to gather the finest fruits and honey, to find the sweetest water. He learned to know the flowers, and he learned the language of the birds. His mind was full of the wonders of nature.

In this way Hemanto and Basanto lived far apart, the days went by, and neither brother knew where the other might be.

When Suworani laughed at the bloodstained robes of the young princes, the royal throne of Rajpur began to tremble. For three days and three nights it shook so violently that the frightened people fled the palace. The despondent raja retired to the forest and became a hermit. Suworani and her three sons were unable to survive in the deserted palace. They wandered for days until they came to the edge of the sea. Suddenly the sky split open, Suworani vanished, and her three sons were swept into the sea.

DAY AFTER DAY the parrot-rani watched the little princess grow into a maiden so beautiful that suitors came from far lands, wooing her with rich gifts. The princess wanted none of them. One day, as she combed her hair with a silver comb, she said to her parrot, "Dear bird, if I do not want golden anklets, or peacock's feathers, or ivory bangles, or jewels for my hair, what *do* I want?"

The parrot-rani answered, "You want the Gojmati."

The princess sprang up, kissed her parrot, threw off all her jewels, and said, "Of course! Of course! I will marry the prince who brings me the Gojmati!" The news was announced in all the kingdoms.

Princes from the seven seas tried to find the wonderful jewel. All of them failed. Even the Raja Hemanto failed to find the Gojmati, and because he could not win Princess Rupobati for himself, he captured her kingdom and ordered his soldiers to lock the gates so that no one else might have her. The princess became Hemanto's prisoner.

IN THE FOREST, Basanto had no news of the world outside. One day a pair of myna birds sat on the roof of the hermit's hut, and Basanto heard them as they talked to each other. The shuk said to the sharee, "Everyone is talking about the great Raja Hemanto who has brought renown to his country. Yet his beautiful prisoner will wed only the prince who brings her the Gojmati."

The shuk replied, "But we alone know where to find the Gojmati. In the Milky Ocean, by the milk white cliffs, thousands and thousands of lotus blossoms live in the glow of the Gojmati's light, unfolding their petals to Golden Lotus, who plays in their midst."

Upon hearing this, Basanto said, "Dear shuk and sharee, dear Uncle and Aunt, what you are saying is wonderful indeed! I shall now find Golden Lotus and the Gojmati."

The shuk and sharee said, "Those are bold words, young hermit. How will you succeed where so many princes have failed?"

Basanto said, "I will not fail."

The shuk said, "Then take with you the muni's trident."

The sharee said, "Your royal robes and your turban are hidden in the shimul tree. You must wear them."

Basanto went to the muni and said, "Father, I am going in search of the Gojmati."

The muni said, "Take my trident." Basanto touched the muni's feet respectfully; then, carrying the trident, he found his royal robes and his turban in the shimul tree and set off in search of the Sea of Milk.

For twelve years he traveled over many hills, through many forests, in many lands. The thirteenth year he saw a marvelous crest of white-crowned rocks from which sprang a milky waterfall. After climbing to the top of the crest, he saw a Sea of Milk in which waves of cream lapped gently amid thousands of lotuses. Playing among the lotuses was a dazzling white elephant. In the center of its forehead was—the Gojmati!

Light from the wonderful jewel glowed like a thousand moons. Basanto stood spellbound. Then, trident in hand, royal robes billowing, he leaped onto the elephant's back and plucked the Gojmati from its forehead. Instantly the milk white elephant turned into a golden lotus, and the Milky Ocean became a sea of pure white sand. Golden Lotus asked, "In what country are you a prince?"

Basanto answered, "I live in a forest, and my guru is a muni."

Golden Lotus said, "Place the Gojmati in your turban, wear me on your robe, and you will find the way to the kingdom of Princess Rupobati."

Standing on the pure white sands of the Milky Ocean,

Basanto fixed Golden Lotus onto his robe and placed the Gojmati in the center of his turban. As he picked up the trident and turned to walk away, voices from beneath the sand called, "Brother! Brother! Take us with you!" Using the trident, Basanto dug in the sand and found three golden fish. He took them with him. The light of the Gojmati showed him the road to follow.

People said, "Look! Look! A god is passing by!"

The radiance of the Gojmati led Basanto directly to the gates of Princess Rupobati's kingdom. People came hurrying to the gates to see the prince who held the luminous jewel. Respectfully they asked, "What prince is this who has come to our kingdom?"

Basanto answered, "I am Prince Basanto from the kingdom of Rajpur. I have brought the Gojmati to your princess."

The people cheered, but they then cried, "The gates of our kingdom are locked! Our princess is Raja Hemanto's prisoner!"

Basanto went straightaway to the kingdom of Raja Hemanto. He sent the three golden fish as a gift to the raja, and with them he sent this message: "The gates of the kingdom of Princess Rupobati must be opened. I have brought the Gojmati." The messenger returned, bowed, and said, "Your worship, our kingdom bids you welcome. After you have refreshed yourself, the raja will receive you."

Hemanto's old nurse began to prepare the beautiful fish which the royal guest had brought. As she was about to cut them open, the fish cried out, "Do not destroy us, Aunt! The raja's brother has brought us!" The astonished nurse ran to the raja with the news. Hemanto at once sent for the prince who had brought the fish. Basanto was taken to him.

Basanto said, "Brother!"

Hemanto said, "Brother!"

The brothers embraced, saying, "Because of Suworani, Duworani's sons have been apart these many years."

At these words the three golden fish turned into three princes. They bowed to Basanto and Hemanto and said, "Brothers, we are the three sons of Suworani. We hope that you will forgive the things that our mother did."

Then the five brothers embraced one another, and Hemanto and Basanto asked what had become of their father, the raja, and of Suworani. The three princes said, "How can we tell you of these sad things? Our father has returned to the forest and become a hermit, and Suworani disappeared at the time that we were swallowed by the sea." The five brothers sat together and talked of many things as the sky turned from purple and gold to the deep blue of midnight.

THE GOLDEN PARROT whirled over and over on her golden perch and said a riddle for the princess: "The wealth of the seven seas is coming to my treasure."

The princess said, "What are you saying, my golden bird?"

The parrot said, "The Gojmati is found, and my spell will soon be broken!" Just then the ayah ran in with the news that the prince who had brought the Gojmati was the brother of Raja Hemanto!

When Princess Rupobati heard this, she kissed her parrot on the beak and said, "Dear Ayah, bring milk from a golden cow. Bring a new yellow bowl. I will bathe my parrot!" The

ayah brought milk and a new yellow bowl. The princess spread a towel on a silver stool and began to bathe the parrot. As soon as she rubbed milk into the top of its head, the magic pellet was dislodged, light filled the room, the parrot's feathers fell away, and Duworani was herself again.

The princess could not believe her eyes. Fearfully she said, "Oh, Rani, I am most afraid! You are so radiant, so like a goddess. What spell has kept you as a parrot these many long years?"

Duworani said, "The spell is now broken, dear Rupobati. The Raja Hemanto is my son. Prince Basanto, who has brought the Gojmati, is also my son." The princess could only bow her head in silent joy.

The next day the princess sent this message to Raja Hemanto: "When the gates of my kingdom are opened, I will come to welcome the bridegroom who has brought the Gojmati." The raja ordered the sepoys to open the gates. He then sent his royal retinue and troupes of musicians to escort Princess Rupobati's palanquin five times around the kingdom. When she arrived at the gates of Hemanto's palace, banners were flying, drums were sounding, and the city was agog with preparations for the betrothal of Princess Rupobati and Prince Basanto.

Hemanto and Basanto were seated on a dais in the royal courtyard. On a blue velvet cushion on a golden tray, the Gojmati glowed in the center of Golden Lotus. The palanquin of Princess Rupobati was brought in and was set before the dais. The princess was screened from view by a curtain of peacock feathers. When the curtain was drawn aside, it could be seen that a lady of incomparable beauty was seated beside the princess. There was a breathless silence.

Hemanto rose from the throne. "Mother!"

Basanto sprang to his feet. "Mother!"

The sons of Suworani exclaimed, "Duworani!" They all surged forward. There was much laughing and weeping. And from his forest retreat the raja arrived and embraced his family.

The goldsmith had fashioned an exquisite chain on which the Gojmati was hung. Basanto slipped the chain over the head of Princess Rupobati. The wonderful jewel illumined the entire city. Then the three kingdoms were united into one, and in the new Rajpur, Duworani, the old raja, Hemanto, Basanto, Princess Rupobati, and Suworani's three sons all began their happy lives together.

The Pomegranate Prince

A HIDEOUS RAKHOSHI had made a nest for herself in the top of the tallest palm tree in the courtyard of the royal palace of Rajpur. Her plan was to eat the rani of Rajpur, take on the rani's bodily form, and replace her in the royal household. As rani she would have servants to wait upon her, yet she could still change herself into a rakhoshi each night and go in search of human flesh. She knew that the rani's life force lay in Prince Kumar's dice, so she crouched in her nest in the palm tree and waited, watching every move that was made in the palace.

One day when the raja was out hunting, Kumar invited five of his friends to play dice with him in the courtyard. The rakhoshi quickly disguised herself as an old beggarwoman and challenged Kumar to gamble with her for possession of the dice.

The boy could not refuse the request of a beggar, and of course he had no way of knowing the power of the dice. He lost possession of them at once, and at the very moment he handed the dice to the rakhoshi his mother fainted. The rakhoshi hastened to the rani's room, ate the rani, assumed her form, and dressed herself in the rani's clothes.

When the raja returned from the hunt, he was not aware of any change in the rani, but Kumar was covered with gooseflesh whenever he came near the false rani, and he noticed that there were often drops of saliva on the tip of her tongue. He kept his thoughts to himself, but he avoided her company. He also saw that the tallest palm tree in the courtyard had begun to wither and that no birds ever lighted on its branches.

IN THE NEXT SEVEN YEARS the false rani had seven sons. When they came of age, they went to the raja and said, "Father, we would like to go on our Desh-bhromon." In those times it was customary for young men of noble birth, on coming of age, to ride forth throughout the kingdom on a journey of exploration and adventure, a Desh-bhromon. The raja gave his consent but said, "Your brother has not yet had his Desh-bhromon, and it is fitting that he should go with you." Each of the eight princes was given a splendid winged horse, a pakhiraj. In a few days the eight princes rode once around Rajpur, then cantered out through the gates of the city to see the world.

The rakhoshi-rani had gone to the palace roof to watch her seven sons as they departed on their journey. When she saw that Kumar was with them, she was extremely angry, for she had planned to get rid of him so that her own sons would inherit the kingdom. She ran swiftly to her room and opened a small casket. Inside the casket was a coiled snake as fine and slender as a silken thread. She said to the snake:

"Oh, slender snake, thy voice
is like the sound of a conch shell.
Speak, and tell me, what is the key
to Kumar's life?"

A voice like the sound of a conch shell, faint as a puff of wind, answered:

"Who knows the key to your life or my life?
But the key to Kumar's life is in the pomegranate seed."

The false rani returned to the roof of the palace and, holding the thread-snake in her hand, said:

"Carried by the wind, then, go!
Make your way to the Realm of Death.
To Pashaboti in the Dice Room there
transmit these words: My seven sons
need seven brides. The rani's son
can kill us all. Eat him alive."

Having released the snake into a strong wind, she then ran to the garden and picked up a pomegranate seed. Holding the seed in her hand, she said this mantra:

"Flying horses! Pakhiraj!
Fly to Pashaboti's land.
There you will find sweet grass.
There you will find cool water."

Then with the seed in her hand she ran to the Thousand Stairs at the edge of the city of Rajpur and said, "Great Stairs, to whom do you belong?" The stairs answered, "To whosoever stands atop the stairway." Climbing to the highest step, the rakhoshi said:

"Then divide yourself in two,
and in the crack
receive and hide this seed."

The stairs opened, embraced the pomegranate seed like a friend, and closed again. Certain that all her plans would now succeed, the false rani retired to her milk white bed and went to sleep.

THE EIGHT PRINCES had bivouacked for the night in the middle of a forest and were sound alseep. At the moment when the pomegranate seed was sealed into the Thousand Stairs, Kumar awoke with a blinding pain in his head. "A scorpion has stung me! Take care!" he shouted. Then he fainted. At the same time a fierce tempest arose, and the lashing wind and rain raging through the forest awakened the seven brothers. Leaning into the wind, they mounted their pakhiraj and flew swiftly away to ride out of the storm. They did not realize that Kumar was not with them.

THE SLEEPING RAKHOSHI had a curious dream. She saw the conch-shell snake being blown toward the river of Yama, the

God of Death. As night fell, the snake sought a place to stop. It drifted over an orchard and came to rest on a luscious mango. It coiled itself inside the ripe fruit and went to sleep. It so happened that mangoes from that very tree were the favorite fruit of the princess of the land, and each night the gardener brought the finest one for her to eat before she retired. This night she ate the fruit in which the thread-snake slept. The rakhoshi knew that the princess had swallowed the snake and that her message would not reach the Realm of Death.

THE SEVEN BROTHERS rode their horses out of the storm. When they saw that Kumar was not with them, they slackened their reins and waited for him to appear. After some time one of the princes said, "Perhaps he has gone ahead and is waiting for us." They asked their horses to find Kumar's pakhiraj. But the seven horses were under the spell of the rakhoshi's mantra and could fly only to Pashaboti's land in the Realm of Death.

When they arrived, Pashaboti and six of her rakhoshi sisters had taken the form of beautiful young women and were sitting at the gateway of the great Dice Chamber. Here victims were lured to gamble for their lives. Gay banners were flying. After exchanging ceremonies of greeting, the brothers said, "Let us have a game of dice. If you lose, we will have you and your six sisters as our brides!"

Pashaboti said, "Who are you?"

"We are princes of Rajpur, and we are on our Deshbhromon."

Aside to her sisters Pashaboti said, "They smell more like

rakhoshes than like humans." To the princes she said, "Do you know the terms of our wager?"

"We do not."

"If you win the game, you will receive the garlands of bridegrooms. If you lose, you will be eaten alive."

The princes said, "Let us begin the game."

Pashaboti said, "First you must give me the message from my kinswoman."

The princes looked at one another in bewilderment and said, "What message? What kinswoman? We have no message." The game was played, and the brothers lost. The seven sisters ate the seven brothers and their seven pakhiraj one by one. Then: haloom! haloom! The sisters all resumed their true forms as rakhoshis. The rakhoshi-rani saw all these things in her dream. She knew that her seven sons had vanished from the human world.

WHEN KUMAR CAME TO HIS SENSES, he climbed on his pakhiraj and flew in search of his brothers. But he was still so dizzy that the bridle fell from his hand, and he slipped from the saddle and glided downward to the earth. The horse landed on a nearby hill and immediately turned to stone. They had fallen into a land called the Night Kingdom. Its raja had died, so that the realm was without a ruler. Each day at noon the royal elephant selected a brave young hero who would be married to the raja's daughter and would become the new sovereign. Each night the princess was married amid great rejoicing. But the next morning nothing remained of the bridegroom but a pile of bones, and the sleeping princess knew nothing of what had happened.

Kumar had landed on the road leading into the city. It was nearly noontime. Bugles and drums sounded; flutes played; banners flew from the gates and the turrets. At noon the royal elephant was led from the stable, carrying on its back the empty throne. People stood in rows along the road, not daring to breathe, for one man among them, soldier, minister, brahmin, or official, would be lifted to the throne. Then conch shells would be blown to announce that a new ruler had been chosen, evening would come, and he would be married to the princess. There would be joyous celebration throughout the night. But everyone knew that in the morning only the sleeping princess would be found in the royal chamber and that in the corner there would be a pile of bones and a few shreds of clothing.

The elephant walked along the road, and people shouted, "Clear the way! Stay in line!" Kumar heard the shouting, but he did not understand. The elephant came to Kumar and stopped. The people stared as the stranger wearing royal robes was lifted to the throne. Then with jubilant shouts everyone went to the palace, and after ceremonial bathing, with incense burning according to the royal rites, Kumar was crowned raja of the Night Kingdom. At dusk he was married to the princess.

When the celebrations were over, the people went to sleep. No one guarded the gates. What was the use? Sentinels and guards had never seen anyone enter or leave. In the whole town there was no sound. Only Kumar was awake.

In the royal chamber the princess had fallen into a deep slumber. The palace was silent. The sky was overcast, and there was no moon. Kumar could see nothing at all. He knew only that the princess lay as though carved of wood, in a sleep so profound that he could not rouse her. Suddenly there was a blaze of light; the princess screamed in her sleep; then the room was again plunged into total darkness. Kumar became aware of a presence. His skin was covered with gooseflesh. Holding his sword firmly, he knelt on one knee and said, "Who is in this room?" He could not see that a snake as fine as a silken thread was emerging from one of the nostrils of the princess; waving its head, the creature soon became as thick as a cord, then it branched out into a monstrous serpent with sixteen heads.

The voice of the snake came softly at first; then with the echoing roar of a great conch shell it swelled until the whole room vibrated with sound. Kumar said, "Whether you are of human flesh or have the black blood of a demon, I will cut you down." The great snake writhed and hissed, spitting fire and venom from thirty-two fangs. Kumar whirled his sword around and around without stopping, and one of the serpent's heads was severed. Instantly the room was flooded with light, and the great snake was blinded. Kumar swiftly cut the creature into seven pieces.

In Rajpur at that very moment the Thousand Stairs began to rumble and crack with the terrible sound of an earthquake. The terrified rakhoshi-rani turned herself into a mouse, squealed with fright, and scurried into the underworld.

From the ruins of the Thousand Stairs a golden pomegranate tree sprouted and spread a thousand branches into the sky. At the moment when the rakhoshi turned herself into a mouse,

the true rani came back to life in her own room, but she remained in a deep sleep.

MEANWHILE, IN THE NIGHT KINGDOM the courtiers crept fearfully to the royal bedchamber and pushed aside the heavy curtains. Behold! There were their new raja and their princess, who was just wakening from a dreamless sleep. Joyfully they cried, "Oh, Raja! Oh, Princess! Rejoice! We are no longer a Night Kingdom!" They saw the devastation in the room and looked with awe upon the body of the great serpent that had been cut into seven pieces. They marveled at the strength of their raja. "Let us burn the snake," they said. As the snake began to burn, the message of the rakhoshi rose from its smoking entrails.

The new raja heard the words and knew at once what had happened to his brothers. He said to the princess, "I must go at once to Pashaboti's land and find my seven brothers. They have been devoured by rakhoshis. Soon I will return." The people of the kingdom stood along the road to wish him well.

Raja Kumar ran to the hill where his pakhiraj had turned to stone. As soon as he touched the noble horse, it came back to life. Kumar leaped to the saddle, saying, "Chee! Chee!" and the horse rose into the air and flew swiftly toward the Realm of Death. When they reached the edge of the realm, it was completely dark, but the pakhiraj continued to fly so swiftly that the stones of the earth beneath were churned into the air.

After a great distance they came to a mountain of cowrie

shells which blocked their way. Kumar shouted, "Pakhi! Do not stop! Hurry!" At first the horse's hooves slipped and skidded on the shells, but as he gathered speed, the shells were turned to dust. Then they came to a mountain of skulls and bones. The teeth of the skulls clicked, and the bones rattled, and beneath the monstrous mountain could be heard the gurgling of a river of blood. Kumar said, "Do not be afraid, Pakhi. Close your eyes and forge ahead!" The horse again gathered speed, and its hooves turned the mountain of bones to powder. At dawn the gates of the Dice Chamber could be seen in the distance.

Pashaboti had again taken the form of a princess and was seated beside the gate. These words were written on the banners that flew in front of the Dice Chamber: "Whoever wins a game from me will win seven brides." Kumar called, "I have come to take up the wager." As they took their positions and prepared to play, Kumar was amazed to find that they were playing with his own dice. He thought that he could not lose, yet he began to lose on the very first throw. Then he noticed that a tiny mouse was cleverly turning the dice over so that he would lose and Pashaboti would win. He sat still for a moment.

Pashaboti became impatient and said, "Come, Prince, make your wager."

But Kumar was thinking. He stood up and said, "Take my horse as a hostage. Tomorrow I will play again." He took his leave. The rakhoshi feasted on his noble pakhiraj.

Early the next morning Kumar went to a nearby village market and bought a kitten. After putting the kitten in his pocket, he went back to the Dice Chamber, took his position, and said, "I am ready to play." As soon as the game began, the mouse crept toward the dice. Kumar released the kitten and the mouse skittered out of sight. Pashaboti lost the first throw. The prince said, "Give me my pakhiraj." Pashaboti gave it to him. Again the dice fell; again she lost. "Give me a prince like myself and a horse like my horse." Pashaboti gave him one of his brothers and his brother's winged horse. They played again and again until all seven princes and all seven pakhiraj were restored. Kumar said, "You may have one more chance. I will play you for the mouse." Pashaboti lost. The kitten pounced on the mouse and ate it up. All the rakhoshis immediately turned into earthworms.

The dice then spoke to Kumar: "Prince, you and your brothers must return to Rajpur before you go back to your new kingdom." With a great whooshing of wings the eight pakhiraj rose into the air and flew homeward to Rajpur.

In Rajpur the rani had revived as soon as the dice were in Kumar's hands. The raja and rani went to the veranda and looked out toward the gates of the city. The road into Rajpur was a cloud of golden dust. Drums were beating a great welcome, and eight princes astride their winged horses could be seen trotting forward in single file. The people along the roadway welcomed the brothers home from their Desh-bhromon. Kumar asked, "Where is my mother?"

The bewildered rani was soon surrounded by eight princes. Kumar told her all that had happened. The raja listened and was astonished. After a great durbar, at which all the events were recounted to the people, Kumar took his leave in order to rejoin his new bride in his own kingdom.

As he rode through the city gates, the withered palm tree split from the roots to the top and crashed into splinters. And when he rode past the Thousand Stairs, the golden pomegranate tree shook its branches in the sunlight and burst into a thousand blossoms.

GLOSSARY

ayah—nursemaid or lady's maid

bengoma birds—mythical birds, always in pairs, male and female

betel nut—nut of the areca palm tree, called betel nut because it is shredded, mixed with lime juice, and wrapped in a leaf of the aromatic betel plant to be chewed like chewing gum

brahmin—member of the highest, priestly caste of Hindus

champa, or champaka—tree of the magnolia family with large, waxy, fragrant flowers from which oil is extracted for perfumes and attars

cowrie shells—beautiful glossy, oval shells of snails abundant on Indian Ocean shores and once used as money

desh-bhromon—literally country-rotation-journey, a journey of exploration of one's country formerly prescribed as the culmination of the coming-of-age ceremony of a princeling

durba grass—a grass sacred for its juices which have medicinal properties for bleeding, wounds, and hysteria

durbar—a public audience held by a raja

evil eye—powerful superstitious belief that evil forces empower certain persons to inflict harm or death by a look

ghat—steps leading down to a landing place on a river, lake, or seashore

guru—honorary title for a revered teacher or mentor

lascar—a sailor

mantra—a prayer or incantation which puts thoughts into words and is sacred to the divinity addressed

mohur—a coin

muni—a hermit who has retired from the world to lead a holy life

pakhiraj—literally "royal bird," legendary winged horses presented to royal princes when they reached manhood

palanquin—a covered litter, usually for one person, carried by four men by means of poles projecting in front and behind

rakhosh, rakhoshi (often rakshasha, rakshashi)—male and female flesh-eating demons who lived in colonies, could transform themselves into any size or shape of living thing, frequently took human form to carry out their evil plans

sepoy—a soldier